ALIVE

A PLAY

By

Jeremiah Alienyi

You're permitted to use this play for stage play, whether it is in your church, school, or other events. However, you should contact the author or publisher first if you want to turn it into a screenplay and produce it as a short film.

Published by

Pearly Gate Media

@pearlygatemedia

88/89 Fesmal Place Peter Odili Rd,

Port Harcourt, River State

Email: pearlymedia@gmail.com

+2348168844527

KDP ISBN: 9798359145169

DEDICATION

For both the inspiration and the grace to put it into writing, I dedicate this book to God Almighty.

CAST

Obinna	A slow learner and introvert
Chika	A bully and Obinna's Classmate
John	A gentle and kindhearted classmate of Obinna
Teacher	Chika's father
Students	Obinna's Classmates
Ife	A friendly neighbour and friend of Obinna
Woman	Provision store owner
Doctor	

SCENE ONE

The scene opens in a classroom. A student with a shaved head that resembles a rock is surrounded by a group of boys. They chatter loudly.

Other students are reading or resting their heads on the desk.

As a teacher enters the classroom, the boys scurry to their seats.

TEACHER: I just got the average scores on your last test. John had the highest score. He scored 85%. A round of applause for him...

The students clap their hands.

TEACHER: (Looks around) Where is Obinna the dummy?

STUDENTS: (Point at a student at the back of the class) He's here sir!

Obinna is mocked by his teacher.

TEACHER: Get up, you dummy! Your performance is getting worse by the day. You are the most stupid student I have ever had. What is it about your brain that prevents you from using it to remember basic information? Your brain works like a sieve; it filters out useful information while holding onto the useless stuff. Your parents are simply wasting their money because you will never be successful in school. You are a dunderhead and a disgrace! (He hisses and leaves the classroom.)

Obinna fights back tears from his eyes as he goes to sit and think by the corridor, outside his classroom.

A student rings the bell.

STUDENT: Closing time!

The students gather their belongings and begin to leave the classroom. They walk past Obinna, who is sitting by the corridor, ignoring him. Chika halts where Obinna is seated and casts him a scornful glance.

CHIKA: (Smacks him on the head) You are so dull. You can never make it! (He laughs at him and walks away.)

Chika smacks Obinna on the head

John packs his books neatly inside his bag and walks up to Obinna. He is putting on glasses and appears friendly.

JOHN: Don't mind what they say about you Obinna. You're not a stupid person. You're intelligent. Just work harder... (Before leaving, he pats him on the back.)

Obinna goes to pick up his bag and leave for home.

<h1 style="text-align:center">SCENE TWO</h1>

Obinna stops by the shop of a woman selling provisions.

Obinna buying rat poison

OBINNA: Ma, I want to buy a poison

WOMAN: Which kind of poison?

OBINNA: Any poison that can kill

WOMAN: Who asked you to buy poison? Do you mean rat poison?

OBINNA: Yes ma. That kills faster.

WOMAN: Okay. It is 200 naira.

Obinna reaches into his pocket and pulls out a 500 naira note. He hands it to her.

WOMAN: (Returns with the rat poison and gives it to him) This is it. By the way, how much is your change?

OBINNA: 150 naira?

WOMAN: How can your change be 150 naira, *Olodo*? Your change is 300 naira! Fine boy like you without brain. *(She presses the change into his palm)* Take!

SCENE THREE

Obinna is back home from school. He doesn't meet anyone, so he quickly takes out the rat poison from his bag. He sits on one of the sofa chairs and brings the poison close to his mouth.

OBINNA: (Soliloquizing) God, if you know you love me and I am not born by mistake, then stop me from taking my life right now!

As he raises the poison to drink it, he hears a knock. He quickly hides it behind the chair.

OBINNA: Who is that? come in.

A knock interrupts Obinna.

The door opens and a young fellow, Ife, about Obinna's age walks in.

IFE: (Cheerfully) How far, Obinna? How are you?

OBINNA: I didn't see you in school today, Ife, what happened?

IFE: Yes. I was a bit down, and I went to the hospital for a test.

OBINNA: Okay. Please go, I want to be alone now.

IFE: Okay, sorry for disturbing you… (He exits and shuts the door behind him)

Obinna lets out a sigh and brings out the poison from where it was hidden. Just as he is about to drink the poison again, he hears a knock on the door. He hides it quickly, frowning.

OBINNA: Who is that?

IFE: (Walks in) Sorry, I wanted to tell you I am hungry. Do you have anything in the house you can give me?

OBINNA: (Pushing Ife towards the door) Please go, there is no food in the house…

Obinna pushing Ife out of his house

After sending him away, he brings out the poison again. As he is about to drink the poison, he hears a knock again.

Before he could hide the poison, Ife enters.

IFE: Your mum said I should tell you she left your food in the warmer.

OBINNA: Okay, thank you. You can leave now.

IFE: There is love in sharing o… (His gaze falls on the rat poison in his hand) Is that not rat poison?

OBINNA: Yes, it is. So what?

IFE: Please can I get a little to use at home? There are too many rats in our house…

Ife tries to collect the poison from Obinna's hand, but Obinna resists him. As Ife struggles to collect the poison, a piece of paper falls from his pocket.

Before Ife can snatch it, Obinna bends and picks it.

OBINNA: (After examining it, he looks up from the piece of paper, shocked.) Ife, what is this?... You have cancer?

IFE: Yes.

OBINNA: How? ... Why? ... When? No... You're a child of God. Why would a good God allow this to happen to you?

IFE: I don't know, but I believe He allowed this to happen to me for a purpose.

OBINNA: What are you saying? What purpose? This is a death sentence, and you're not even showing any concern. Are you normal?

IFE: I doubted God's love for me when I was diagnosed with cancer, but I am reassured of His love for me. Just imagine I was a clay vessel and the potter decides to break me. Will I accuse him of being evil? Of course, I won't because He is my Creator, and I believe if He decides to break me, it's because He wants to make me a better person.

Isaiah chapter 55:9 says, *"For as the heavens are higher than the earth, so are my ways higher than your ways, and my thoughts than your thoughts."*

Obinna falls to his knees and begins to cry.

Obinna, don't worry, God is in control.

Obinna on his knees crying

OBINNA: Ife, you just saved me from taking my life!

IFE: What do you mean?!

OBINNA: I couldn't take the abuses anymore. Everyone says I am stupid and calls me a dummy; that I will not make it in life. I wanted to drink this poison and end it all.

IFE: (Shocked) What? God!... Thank you, Jesus! ... Obinna, you shall not die but live to fulfil the purpose of God in your life. (Ife offers his hand) Let's pray...

As they are praying, Ife's phone rings. They finish praying and Ife picks up the call.

IFE: Hello...

DOCTOR: (O.S) Hello. Is that Ife on the line? The result of the test given to you isn't yours. Please look at it again. What name is there?

IFE: (Checks the result again, carefully) Ife Daba. I think there is a mistake with the name. My name is Ife Ekundayo

DOCTOR: Yes, the nurse just brought yours. I am sorry for the mistake.

IFE: Oh, it's okay. Is mine different from this?

DOCTOR: I don't know how to explain this, but the test shows no trace of cancer anymore. Ife, you're cancer-free. Your cancer is gone!

Ife jumps up in excitement...

IFE: I AM CANCER FREE!!!

OBINNA: (Dazed) What?!

IFE: I'M CANCER-FREE!!!

He runs out of the room happy...

Black Out

SCENE FOUR

NARRATOR: (O.S) A FEW MONTHS LATER

In the classroom.

The teacher comes in.

TEACHER: A miracle just happened. Obinna, had the highest score in the just concluded test. He had 90%.

The students are filled with amazement as they applaud him.

TEACHER: Okay, that's enough... The last position is …
(pauses and casts an angry glance at Chika)
Chika, come here!

He takes him to a corner outside of the classroom.

The teacher is disappointed in his son, Chika

TEACHER: Chika, how come you are last in your class? What do you want everyone to think of me, Chika? You're my son for goodness sake. Why are you bringing disgrace to me? Why did you come last in the class? ... Can't you talk?! .... You will see pepper today when you get home. Go back to your class you dummy!

He walks out of his presence as the closing bell rings.

John goes to meet Obinna while other students leave the classroom...

OBINNA: (V.O) God's love kept me alive. He has restored my memory and given me reasons to live again. Don't give up on God. He loves you. He's your heavenly Father. If you pray to Him and obey His instructions, He will help you.

John put his hand around Obinna's shoulder as they walk out of the stage.

Black Out

19

EPILOGUE

There are lots of troubles in this world. Some people don't have food to eat. Some people don't have good clothes on their backs or a roof over their heads. Scattered all over the world are also people who are living from hand to mouth. Many are also plagued with all kinds of diseases.

Not only do the poor face difficulties; but the wealthy also face difficulties. That is why you may have heard of a doctor packing his car and jumping over the lagoon. It was not a lack of money that drove him to jump over the lagoon and commit suicide. He is wealthy. He owns a car. He has a good job and an enviable profession, but unfortunately, none of those things could shield him from life's storms.

Trouble comes in different forms and shapes. In the case of Obinna, it was emotional and psychological trouble. He was mocked and abused because he wasn't as brilliant as his classmates. He was the laughingstock of his class and a shame to his school.

This made him depressed, and he decided to end his life by suicide.

His story is similar to that of many of us who are thinking about suicide or are on the verge of giving up on life due to life's troubles. We believe that death is the only way out of all of our problems and traumas, but this is not the case. Jesus is the only way out. He is the truth, the way, and the life.

Because of sin, the world is full of evil and trouble, which is why Jesus came to die for us so that we might be free from the power and consequences of sin.

In Matthew chapter 11 verses 28-30, He tells us how to weather life's storms and troubles.

> *Come to Me, all you who labor and are heavy laden, and I will give you rest.*
>
> *Take My yoke upon you and learn from Me, for I am gentle and lowly in heart, and you will find rest for your souls.*
>
> *For My yoke is easy and My burden is light.*

To come to Jesus means to be born again or to be saved

> *"That if you confess with your mouth the Lord Jesus and believe in your heart that God has raised Him from the dead, you will be saved."* **Romans 10:9**

After being born again, He says you should take His yoke upon you and learn from Him. This means two things. First, you must be prepared to face the challenges that come with being born again, which will ultimately work out for our good.

> *"Then He said to them all, "If anyone desires to come after Me, let him deny himself, and take up his cross daily, and follow Me"* **Luke 9:23**
>
> *"For our light affliction, which is but for a moment, is working for us a far more exceeding and eternal weight of glory"* **2 Corinthians 4:17**

Secondly, you must study His word and follow in His footsteps

> *"Looking unto Jesus, the author and finisher of*

*our faith, who for the joy that was set before Him
endured the cross, despising the shame, and has
sat down at the right hand of the throne of God."*
Hebrews 12:2

When you follow through on these, then you will receive the promise of rest and you won't be weighed down by the troubles of life. He will be with you and lead you out of all your troubles, just like He did for Obinna in our play.

QUESTION

1. Who is the dummy in Scene one?

2. Why did Obinna want to kill himself?

3. How did God hear Obinna and stop him from committing suicide?

4. Why does God sometimes allow seemingly evil things to happen to His children?

5. How do people contribute to the rate of suicide in our society?

6. Who is the dummy in Scene four?

NOTE

NOTE

NOTE

NOTE